THE
WILD KID

THE WILD KID

HARRY MAZER

ALADDIN PAPERBACKS

NEW YORK   LONDON   TORONTO   SYDNEY   SINGAPORE

First Aladdin Paperbacks edition July 2000

ALADDIN PAPERBACKS
An imprint of Simon & Schuster Children's Publishing Division
1230 Avenue of the Americas
New York, NY 10020

Also available in a Simon & Schuster Books for Young Readers
hardcover edition.

Book design by Heather Wood.
The text for this book was set in Giovanni Book.

Printed and bound in the United States of America.

10 9 8 7 6 5 4 3 2

The Library of Congress has cataloged the hardcover edition as follows:
Mazer, Harry.
The wild kid / Harry Mazer.—1st ed.
p.   cm.
Summary: Twelve-year-old Sammy, who is mildly retarded, runs
away from home and becomes a prisoner of Kevin, a wild kid
living in the woods.
ISBN 0-689-80751-1 (hc.)
[1. Mentally handicapped—Fiction.   2. Runaways—Fiction.   3.
Feral children—Fiction.]   I. Title
PZ7.M47397Wp   1998
[Fic]—dc21   97-42578
ISBN 0-689-82289-8 (Aladdin pbk.)

For my friend Barbara Seaman

—H.M.

THE
WILD KID

The door was locked, and he was outside. It had taken both of them to put him out. His mother couldn't move him alone. He'd clung to the door, and she'd had to call Carl.

She made him sit on the steps. There were five steps down. He counted them. His feet were on the second step.

"Sammy," his mother said. She wanted him to listen to her. "You can't just say things."

His mother said he'd cursed Carl, used a bad word. All he did was say one word. His mother said it. Carl said it all the time. "People look at you," his mother said, "and they see an almost-grown-up person, and they expect you to act like an almost-grown-up person. Do you know what I'm saying, Sammy? You have to think about the words you use."

He knew about words. He had a lot of words. Sometimes the teacher said he talked too many words. He knew about bad words, too. Some words were worse than others. Retard was a worse word than crap. His friend Dennis in school said crap-a-dap all the time. Some kids said crap when they went to the toilet. Say crap backward and it was parc. Say Sammy backward and it said Ymmas.

His mother sat down next to him, close, and held his hand in hers. He kept an eye on her other hand. She hit sometimes. Not in a mean way. Only if he was lazy or wasn't paying attention. Her hand was soft, but it could be hard, too.

"Look at me," she said. She was always extra nice after she was mean to him. He liked it when she sat so close. He could see where she'd plucked her eyebrows. Plucking had made them look fat, like little pillows.

She got up. "Are you listening, Sammy? Would you talk that way to your father? Think about it." She went back inside.

Boy, oh boy. He wouldn't talk that way to his father. He never did. He didn't talk to his father, because his father was dead, and you didn't talk to dead people.

His father's name was Ernest E. Ritchie, and he died a long time ago, on November 16. People said Sammy was slow, but he knew things. His father died on Thursday at four-fifteen o'clock in the morning, one month and two days after Sammy's sixth birthday party. Sammy was twelve years old now, but he was mostly done being twelve years old. In twenty-nine days he would be thirteen years old.

He knew a lot of things. He knew that if you farted in front of people you said, "Excuse me." Carl farted, and Sammy reported that he didn't say excuse me. Carl laughed, but his mother said Sammy had to apologize to Carl for saying he farted, even if he did. Sammy couldn't hold his nose, either, the way he did with his friend Dennis.

Carl liked to wrestle with Sammy. He told Sammy to get a good tight hold around his neck and not let go. Carl's head was bald, and sometimes Sammy would grab on to his ears, but he still was thrown off. As hard as he tried, Sammy could never pull Carl down. Carl would snap his fingers and say, "Hey, man, nothing to it."

Sammy tried to make his fingers snap, too, but no way.

"Lick your fingers first," Carl advised.

Sammy tried and tried. He could pop his tongue better than Dennis, but he couldn't snap his fingers.

Today, Carl was in a bad mood. He snapped his fingers at Sammy. "Get me one of those cold drinks, and snap to it."

The way he said it gave Sammy a pinch in his belly. "Crap to it," he said. The words just popped out. He wasn't cursing Carl. Maybe just a little. He tried to look sorry, but a smile came on his face, anyway.

His mother said he had to apologize, and she put him outside. "Apologize, and you can come back in."

He sat outside on the steps. Why did Carl have to be in their house all the time? Like it was his house. It wasn't his house. It was his mother's house and Sammy's house and his sister Bethan's house. Why did Carl take the couch and nobody else could have it? Why did he snap his fingers at Sammy all the time?

Sammy looked at his watch. It was two-thirteen in the P.M., Sunday, but there was no sun. It was gray, so it should be called Grayday. There was a little sizzle of wet in the air. It wasn't late, but it seemed late because it was so dark and he wanted to be inside.

He practiced saying I'm sorry. "I'm sorry. I'm sorry. I'm sorry. I'm sorry." He said it ten million times till he couldn't say it anymore.

Several times he tried the door, but it was locked on the inside. The garage was open, but the door to the kitchen was locked. He tried the cellar door. He imagined how he would turn the handle silently and slide into the house, and step carefully down the steps into the cellar. There were spiders in the cellar, but he didn't care. Carl was afraid of spiders, but Sammy liked spiders.

Where they lived, there were lots of spiders and lots of houses and lots of fields. Sometimes animals came out at night and knocked over the garbage pails. Once, a big fat raccoon came in the garage and tried to come in through the kitchen door. His sister Bethan saw it and slammed the door. Then they ran to the window and watched the raccoon waddle away.

He got his bike from the garage and put on his helmet. Then he leaned his bike against the house and climbed up on the seat and looked into the living room. Carl was sitting on the couch, stroking his bald head. He shaved his head so he would look like an athlete.

Sammy dropped down and went around to his sister's window and climbed up on the bike seat again. He pressed his face against the glass and flattened his lips so he looked like a goldfish. Bethan came to the window and opened it. Bethan was his little sister and his best sister. Emily used to be his best sister till she went away to college. Now he played with Bethan, and she was in charge when his mother wasn't home.

Bethan hugged him. "You going to say you're sorry to Carl?"

"Pull me in," he shouted.

"Shhh, honey! You want to convince Mom to let you come back in."

"I'll convince her," he shouted.

Bethan tried to pull him in, but she couldn't because he was bigger and heavier than she was.

"You smell like ketchup," he said.

"Oh! Like ketchup?"

"No! Worse! Like mustard. No, like smelly cheese!"

"You're bad!" She was laughing. Then she put her finger to his lips, but it was too late. Their mother had heard and come into Bethan's room.

Sammy ducked his head under the window.

"Why's your window open?" his mother said.

"I'm hot," Bethan said.

His mother looked out the window. "Sammy, are you there? Where are you?" She looked right over his head.

He bit his lip to keep the laughing inside.

"Why does he have to stay outside, Mom?" Bethan said. "It's going to rain."

"He can't be rude to Carl."

"Carl doesn't care. What's so terrible about saying crap, anyway? He didn't even say it to Carl. He said, 'Crap to it.' That's funny, Mom."

"Don't do that," his mother said. "Don't excuse him. You know he has to learn not to just say things and then blow it off. He has to behave properly, or people are not going to like him and he's going to have a harder time in life. He's not just a cute little pup anymore."

His mother looked down and saw him. "Oh, there's my little pup. What a surprise." She scratched his helmet. "Look at you, your shoelaces."

He looked down. "They untied themselves." They both laughed at his funny joke. He started to climb in through the window.

"No, Sammy, I'm serious." He hung on the windowsill. "When you apologize to Uncle Carl, you can come in."

"What time?" he said.

"That's up to you. As soon as you do it."

"What time?"

She looked at his watch. "Say it in two minutes and you can come in."

He watched the second hand go around twice. "Can I come in now? It's two minutes."

"Are you ready to apologize to Uncle Carl?"

She wanted him to say yes. He wanted to, but he still couldn't make his mouth say the words. "He's not my uncle. His name is Carl Torres. My father's name is Ernest E. Ritchie, and my name is Samuel Ernest Ritchie."

"Why are you so stubborn? Carl's my friend, and he's your friend, too. Who plays with you? Carl. Who took you to buy the bike? Carl. Who bought you the special chain? Carl."

"Carl is a big fart." The words jumped out of his mouth.

His mother slapped his face.

He dropped to the ground. His face burned. He wanted to run and hide his face. He wanted to charge into his mother and bite her as hard as he could.

His mother leaned out the window. "I'm sorry I did that, Sammy." Her face had the sorry look, but she still wouldn't let him in. "I don't want to hear that kind of language again from you. I feel ashamed and worried when you talk that way. You're getting too old to just blurt out any words you want to. I want you to pay attention. You can do it. I know you can. As soon as you're ready to say you're sorry, you can come back in." She shut the window.

"I'm never coming back in." It made him feel good to say it, and he said it again. He shouted as loud as he could, "Never, never, never coming back!"

He fastened his helmet. The light went on next door, and Tessie, the cat, came out. "I'm never coming back," he told her, and tears came to his eyes, and he had to squinch them so they wouldn't come out.

2

It started to rain. Just like Bethan said. His sister was smart. A drizzle. It tickled his ears and got down his neck. Nobody was out on the street. Not even cars. He pulled his collar up and rode over to Billy's house. Billy Pryor was his friend. He lived two blocks away, and Sammy could go there.

There were no lights in Billy's house. No car in the driveway. Sammy rode his bike in circles in the driveway. Nobody came out and said, "Oh, it's you, Sammy!" Mrs. Pryor always wanted him to come in and eat something. She said he was too skinny, but his mother said he was just right.

Sammy closed his eyes and made circles and figure eights. He kept hoping Mrs. Pryor would come out. She was nice to him. "Oh, it's Sammy, my favorite boy." Sometimes he loved her more than he did his own mother. She didn't want him to do things all the time. And sometimes she gave him candy bars.

He wanted a candy bar now, and he wanted it real bad. He felt the money in his pocket against his leg as he rode toward Marsden's Market on South Bay Road. He wasn't supposed to go there by himself, but he had money, and he could go there if he wanted to! He knew the way. You went past Billy's house, and then you went three more blocks.

There were just a few cars in Marsden's parking lot. Sammy leaned his bike against a pole by the window. Inside he looked out to make sure his bike was okay. His bike had an aluminum frame with a pale blue stripe, and it sparkled. It was the most beautiful bike in the whole world. He caught a reflection of himself in the glass. His helmet was on crooked, and he adjusted it. Otherwise, people laughed at you. He knew how to do things.

At the checkout counter he bought a candy bar. The checkout girl's head was covered with little ribbons and beads that made him think *candy,* and he said, "Your hair looks like candy." She smiled and showed a dimple in each cheek.

"Would you tie my shoelaces?" he asked.

"What?"

"My shoelaces are untied."

"Can't you tie your own shoelaces?"

"I can, but I make a mess."

She came around the counter and bent down to tie them for him.

"Can I touch the little beads on your head?" He remembered he wasn't allowed to touch people without asking permission.

She let him. He touched three beads. "You are a very nice person," he said.

He went over to the magazine rack and looked at all the different muscle magazines. "Boy, oh boy, what muscles." He tensed his arm. He could feel his muscle wriggling around like a little mouse, not big like in the pictures.

When he went back to the window to check his bike again, it wasn't where he'd left it against the pole. He looked at his watch. It was almost three o'clock. He ran out of the store, thinking he'd left his bike in the wrong place and someone had moved it. Bikes were supposed to be put in the bike rack. "I'm sorry," he said, "I forgot."

The bike rack was near the entrance to the store, but his bike wasn't there, either. He went around to the back of the building. There were wooden skids and flattened boxes and two long brown Dumpsters, but no bike. He ran back inside the store. Somebody could have brought it inside so it wouldn't get wet in the rain.

The nice girl with ribbons in her hair wasn't at the counter. Instead, there was a fat man in short pants. His sneakers were unlaced. He pointed a finger at Sammy. "No running in the store, boy."

"Did you see my bike?" Sammy said. "Did you put it someplace else? Would you please give me my bike?"

"No bikes in the store," the man said.

"Did someone bring my bike in? Did someone do it?" He knew he was talking too loud and too fast.

"No bikes in the store," the man said.

Sammy stared out the window at the pole where his bike had been, then he rushed out again and ran all around, sure that someone had put it someplace where he wasn't looking. "Boy, oh boy," he kept saying. "Oh, my bike, my bike!"

He saw a flash way over by the road at the other end of the parking lot. A bike, his bike! Someone was riding his bike away.

Sammy yelled, "Heyyyy, you!" He had a big voice; he could yell louder than anyone in his class, except for Mrs. Hoffman. He yelled again, "Heyyyyyy you, that's my bike. I didn't give you permission! Bring my bike back."

The bike and rider disappeared down the highway.

Sammy stood at the edge of the road. There was nothing to see. No bike, no rider. His bike had disappeared. He followed the skinny tire prints the wheels had left in the wet mud. He ran as hard as he could. He was a champion swimmer, but just a regular runner.

There were puddles all along the side of the road. He splashed through them, looking ahead, following the tracks. When he caught the stealer, he'd yell at him. He'd say, "You should be ashamed." That's what his mother would say. And then the person would be sorry for doing a bad thing.

Sometimes the tracks disappeared when the bike veered onto the road, but then they'd appear in the mud again.

When he couldn't run anymore, he walked. Automatically, he felt for his helmet. It was gone. It must have fallen off. He didn't have time to go back for it now.

If he came home without his bike, his mother would be

so upset. She'd say, "Oh, Sammy, your new bike!" And maybe she'd cry. Carl would say, "Man, oh man, didn't you have it chained?"

His mother had given him the money for the bike, but Carl had bought him the extra strong chain. "What do you think the chain was for?" Carl would say. "Something to hang around your neck?"

Where was his bike? He kept looking ahead and following the tracks. He had to get his bike back.

Just past a gas station, a truck with high wooden sides was pulled over on the edge of the road. The engine heaved and coughed, the sides shook, and smoke came out the back. The driver was nearby at a food stand. Sammy waited for him next to the truck. He was going to ask for a ride, but when the man came over he had such a mean look, Sammy turned away.

When the truck started to move, Sammy grabbed on to the side and climbed in the back. Loose pieces of lumber bounced on the floor. Sammy knelt by the tailgate, watching out for the tire tracks. The truck went fast, and he was cheering. Pretty soon he'd catch up to the stealer.

As the truck picked up speed, it was harder for Sammy to see the tracks. Sometimes he saw them, sometimes he just thought he saw them. Then he didn't see them at all. He waited for them to appear again. He waited a long time, and then he banged on the roof of the cab.

The truck stopped with a jolt, and Sammy tumbled forward. The driver saw him through the window and yelled. He had little red eyes. He came running around the side of the truck.

Sammy jumped up on top of the cab. Quick. And then slid down on the hood and off the truck.

"Hey, you, I'll break your neck!" The man had a stick in his hand.

Sammy ducked under a guardrail and tumbled down a steep incline. He couldn't stop himself. He crashed into a thicket and lay there, breathing hard. Then he got up and ran again. If the man caught him, he'd arrest him and put him in jail. He banged into a tree. His mouth was open, chest heaving. He ran on. He kept going, deeper into the woods.

Sammy ran on. He fell and got up and ran again. His sneakers were dirty, and his pants had mud on them. When he got home, his mother would tell him to take off all his clothes and take a nice hot bath.

A plane flew over. Sammy heard it and then he saw it. He waved as hard as he could, but the trees were in the way. He remembered the time Carl took him for an airplane ride—just him, not Bethan—and how, as they went higher, everything got smaller and smaller. Tiny houses. Tiny cars. He kept looking for his house.

He leaned against a big tree, pressing his body into it. He felt the tree move, breathing the way he was breathing. It sighed, talking to him, telling him not to worry. His mom worried all the time. "Don't worry, Mom. Worrie-eee…" He sang the word under his breath. Worry Mom. Everything was a worry. "What are you going to wear this morning, Sammy?

Did you get dressed yet? Hop-a-long, cowboy! Did you brush your teeth, honey? Cheerios for breakfast again, don't you want something different? Don't put so much milk in, you'll have a stomachache. Take that sweater off and put on a clean one. Hurry, you'll be late for the school bus."

He found a path. Then he found another path. Then he was all mixed up. Every way, there were trees, trees, trees. He was sick of trees. He wanted to see houses and cars and stores. He wanted his mother and his sister. He even wanted Carl. The time was four thirty-one. He'd better go home fast. His mother would be calling, "Sammy, supper time."

Was he lost? Don't say lost. Lost was bad. He was turned around, was all. Like being spun around in a game and getting all dizzy and mixed up. He just needed to be pointed in the right direction.

Suddenly a bunch of noisy birds flew through the trees. He followed them. They were fast, but then they stopped and yelled at him. Right where he stopped, there were wooden cleats on the tree. He climbed up to a platform and sat there. This was his tree house, where he could stay till someone came for him.

It was raining again. Just a little at first. It was still dry against the trunk. But then it rained harder, and the air was full of wetness. His knees got wet, and his head and the whole platform got wet. Everything was wet; his face was wet all over.

He climbed down and buried into a dark tangle of trees. Rough, stabby branches reached to the ground. They grabbed at him and tore at his jacket, but underneath it was like a room and it was dry.

He sat with his knees drawn up and his collar raised, listening to the soft drip of rain. He broke off little branches and made tiny houses and a street, and he made one branch a car and drove it to his house. Then he made a stick mother and a stick sister. And he jumped out of the car and kissed his stick mother and his stick sister, and they kissed him.

5

Little beeps, like tiny bike horns, woke him. He thought somebody had brought him his bike and was beeping the horn. "Hey!" he said. "Here I am." Branches stuck him as he crawled out. The tree kept hooking him, holding him back. Several big birds with long, skinny necks and little gnarly heads that bopped this way and that flew up into the trees. Turkeys!

He'd never seen real living turkeys before. "Hi, you birds." Sammy waved. He was happy for their company, but they disappeared through the trees.

He stretched and brushed himself off. He'd slept well, not waking once. He'd never slept in the woods before. Wait till he told everybody. Boy, oh boy, I slept in the woods. His mother would be surprised. She never even let him sleep over at Billy's house. She said he'd make too much work for Mrs. Pryor. His watch said five-thirty in the morning. Boy, oh boy.

He never got up this early. That was something else to say to his mother.

He started walking. The ground went up and down, and he went up and down. He liked going down, but then he had to go up.

He found black berries hanging in a tree, and he tasted them. They were like little sour grapes with seeds. He didn't like them, but he ate them because he was hungry.

"Keep walking," he told himself. "That's the way." When he walked, the worry thoughts slipped away.

When he got high enough, on top of the highest hill, he knew he would see something. It would be like the day his whole class went up on the roof of the school. Mrs. Hoffman had explained how you make a map and how you use a compass to know direction. He wished his watch had a compass on it. That way he would never get lost.

Not that he was lost. Lost wasn't a good word, and he didn't use it. He was just a little mixed up. Sort of turned around. He just had to turn himself straight. It was like the time he was little and wandered away and went in the wrong house. "Mommy," he called. A man came, and he looked surprised to see Sammy, and then he laughed and showed him which way to go.

But here in the woods, there were no houses, only trees, leaning together, watching him go by. They were whispering about him, he thought, but he couldn't understand their talk.

Near the edge of a steep ravine, there was a big pine tree with lots of dead branches to hold on to, and he climbed it. He was a good climber. When he got to the top, he was disappointed. It was like looking down at the back of a giant green and brown dog. There were no roads, no shopping mall, not even one little house. Just trees, trees, trees.

The wind blew, and the pine tree swayed. The forest was green and brown, and the sun was hidden behind a white sky. Sammy didn't know what to do next. Maybe another airplane would fly over and see him on top of the tree. Maybe Carl would be looking for him in the airplane. He waited a long time, but no plane came.

It was harder going down the tree than going up, because he had to feel around for the branches with his feet. "Watch your step, Sammy." A branch broke. He lost his footing and slid down too fast. "Hey," he yelled. He grabbed for a branch, but it broke under his weight, and he fell out of the tree and tumbled down an embankment. Down Sammy went. Down, down, down, all the way down.

He was lying next to a pile of brush with a window in it. It looked like a camper window. His friend Billy Pryor's father had a window like that on his camper.

A window in the woods? That was funny.

He saw a face looking through the window. An animal was peering out at him, an animal with long cat eyes.

He backed away, not taking his eyes from the face. He backed and backed, then turned and ran. He dove into a bush and lay still. He heard the animal thing sniffing around. He could smell it.

It reached in, grabbed him by the ankle, and pulled him out. Sammy's face was in the ground. He lay very still. He heard the animal breathing, and he remembered a story of a little boy sitting in the arms of a bear. The boy said, "Don't eat me." So the bear didn't.

"Don't eat me," Sammy said.

"Who the hell are you?"

The animal talked.

"Please don't eat my face," Sammy said.

"Where the hell you come from?"

Sammy opened his eyes a crack. The animal was naked, except for a pair of ragged jeans. But it wasn't an animal. It was a person with a regular face. A tall, skinny kid with long arms and legs.

He turned Sammy over and sat on him. He pinned Sammy's arms with his sharp knees and held his hand over Sammy's mouth. He kept looking all around with his big, dark animal eyes.

Sammy twisted. The wild kid was choking him.

He dragged Sammy through a hole and into a dark place that smelled of dirt and fire and garbage. "Let me go, please," Sammy said.

"Keep your mouth shut!" He had hair on his face and around his chin, like a goat. "Where are they? Who's with you?"

"There's nobody, just me."

The wild kid taped Sammy's hands behind him, then taped his feet together, then his mouth.

Then the wild kid went away. Sammy was alone in the dark, except for the light that filtered through the little window.

Sammy threw himself around. He couldn't breathe and his nose was clogged. The gag stuck to his skin.

He was in a little room, not really a room, more like a cave. Not even a cave. More like a hole scooped out under some rocks. A torn piece of plastic hung over the opening. A scrap of dirty green rug was on the ground, and a mattress and some cardboard boxes and plastic pails.

The wild kid came back. He grabbed Sammy by his jacket, and pushed him into the back of the cave. He knelt on his hands and knees, staring at Sammy, his face so close, Sammy could smell his stinky breath.

Sammy stayed still, afraid to move. The kid went through Sammy's pockets and took his dollars and change. "Who are you?" he asked. He tore the tape off Sammy's mouth. "Where'd you come from? What's your name?"

Sammy licked his lips. "Sammy," he said. "What's your name?"

"How'd you get here?" He had a snake tattoo around his wrist. "Where you from?"

"I got lost. I'm sorry I fell on your house. Let me loose, please. I'll go away, I promise."

"Who sent you?" He talked funny. He had teeth missing.

"Nobody." Sammy shook his head as hard as he could. "Somebody took my bike, and then I got lost. Can I go home now?" Sammy glanced at the snake tattoo. He didn't like snakes. His stomach hurt, and he was sore all over.

The kid pulled a knife from his belt and pointed it at Sammy. "You know what I can do with this?" He drove it down into his own hand.

Sammy gasped, and the kid laughed. "Gotcha!" He had driven the knife between his outspread fingers.

"That's a good trick," Sammy said. He kept licking his lips.

The wild kid stabbed at his spread fingers, again and again, the darting blade coming close, but missing each time. "You ever see anybody do that?"

"No."

"You bet. Nobody's got the nerve, but me. Who else is with you?" he said suddenly.

"Nobody. I told you."

"You're a liar."

"I don't lie. Only bad boys lie."

The kid stared at him with a look that, even in the dimness, Sammy recognized.

"How old are you, anyway?" the kid said.

"I'm twelve. In twenty-eight days I'll be thirteen."

"So, what are you, dumb?"

"No. I'm Down's." Sometimes it was okay to tell, but sometimes people teased. "I'm young for my age. I'm a special person."

"You're a dumb person," the kid said. "Only a dumb person like you would find me."

"Because I lost my bike." Sammy explained how he'd left his bike for five minutes and ten seconds, and how he'd run after the stealer, and about getting in the truck, and being chased into the woods and getting lost and climbing the tree and falling down.

"And then I fell on your house." He wanted to demonstrate the way he'd tripped and tumbled down, but it was hard to do without using his hands and feet. All he could do was yell, "Uh! Oh! Oh!" the way he had yelled falling down the hill.

"You're stupid," the kid said. "You don't leave your bike where somebody can take it. If I saw it, I would have taken it in a minute. You're really dumb."

"I'm not dumb. You can be retarded and not dumb."

"Dumb."

"That's not nice," Sammy said.

"You got it right that time, dummy. I'm a bad guy, so look out, Mr. Goody Boy. I suppose you never did anything bad?"

Sammy said nothing.

"Well, did you?"

Sammy nodded. "Sometimes."

"Right! I got you, you little hypocrite. Don't look at me with those big baby eyes and lie to me. I can tell, just by looking at you, that you lie all the time. Now, you'd better tell me the truth. You going to run away if I untie you?"

"No. I promise."

The kid freed Sammy's hands and then his feet. Sammy rubbed his wrists and his ankles.

"Just remember, you try anything, and I can tie you up again in a second," the kid said. He wadded up the tape and threw it away, then crouched by the entrance, looking out. "What am I going to do with this dumb kid? What's he want?"

Who was he talking to? Sammy crept closer.

"I let him go, and what? He goes back and tells everybody he found this guy in the woods. He starts blabbing about Kevin in the woods, and they say, 'So that's where he is!' And then the whole army and air force and helicopters and search dogs come looking for me. They'll get me and lock me up, and that'll be the end of Kevin. I've got to kill him."

He turned and shoved Sammy into the back again. "You got me in a fix now, dummy!"

"I can go home," Sammy said. "I will. I'll go right straight home."

"You'll be home, and I'll be back at Fieldstone, that rat hole. They're going to say, 'Where'd you get this kid from?' They're going to say I kidnapped you. Anything I tell them, they'll say it's a lie.

"Fieldstone?" Sammy said. "Is that where you live?"

"Fieldstone is where they send me if they catch me. It's a school you can't leave. No way, man. Nobody's grabbing K-Man and locking him up."

8

"Don't even think about going out." Kevin's mattress was right in front of the doorway. He was lying down, hooked up to a tape player. "You want to be tied up again? Get back there."

Sammy had to stay in back. There was a plank he could sit on, but there wasn't enough room to stand up. He was hungry and he had to pee, but he was afraid to say anything.

Kevin lay on his back, and sometimes one foot went up and bounced around and then the other.

"Is that good music?" Sammy asked.

Kevin didn't answer.

Sammy held his watch up to the light. Yesterday, right now, he was home. He was talking to Bethan, trying to climb into her room.

Kevin was eating a Pop-Tart and drinking from a plastic water bottle.

Sammy lay down on the plank. He turned from one side to the other. He couldn't get comfortable. Sammy wished he could go to sleep and wake up in his own bed. He lay on his back like Kevin with his knees bent. He reached up to the ceiling with his feet. He could almost touch it. When he sat up and put his hands over his head, he could touch it.

Kevin was looking at him. "What are you doing?"

"Nothing." Sammy put his hands down and examined them, finger by finger. They were all scratched up and dirty. Kevin had no sink in his house, no faucet; no water, even. When she saw him, his mother would wash his hands and face for him. "People see your dirty face and they say you're a dirty boy. Are you a dirty boy, Sammy?" She liked to wash him, and he only minded when his friends were over.

"I've got to pee," he said.

"Hold it," Kevin said.

"I can't. I've been holding it too long."

Kevin gave him a hateful look. He got up and pushed Sammy out through the narrow opening. "Don't do it around here. And don't get any ideas. I'm watching you."

Sammy found a tree a few steps from the cave. It was a relief to be outside and on his feet.

"Hurry up!" Kevin said.

"I'm really thirsty," Sammy said when they went back in. He sat down on the bench again.

Kevin pointed to a row of plastic water bottles. "Take one. That's yours," he said. "It gets empty, you fill it up."

"Where?"

"Don't worry about it. You'll find out." Kevin opened a metal trunk and took out a box of Pop-Tarts. Sammy smelled them and moved closer. Kevin pushed him away. "Stay on your side!" He ate a Pop-Tart and threw away the box.

It was empty except for some crumbs that Sammy licked up. He drank from his water bottle, then sat there, holding it in his arms.

That night, Kevin tied Sammy up and went out. He left Sammy lying on the ground. It was darker than dark. It was the darkest dark Sammy had ever been in. Darker than being in a closet with the door closed.

There were sounds all around him. Crinkly sounds, like somebody walking toward him. They stopped, and another sound started, like papers being torn into little pieces. He listened; he listened so hard, he thought his ears got as big as TV dishes. Something was moving from one place to another. Inside? *Snakes?* Sammy drew his head in. He wished he was a turtle and could pull his whole self into a safe little house.

"Oh, Mom, where are you?" There was comfort in hearing a voice, any voice. It was his own, Sammy's voice. Kevin said he had to be quiet, but he was talking, anyway.

"I want to go home. I want to see my mother. I want to see

Bethan, my sister. I want to go home." He said it loud. Then louder. Then he shouted it. "I WANT TO GO HOME."

He slept and woke. Hunger kept waking him up. His stomach was eating him. It was so dark, sometimes he didn't know if he was asleep or awake or where the dark ended and he started. He closed his eyes. It was better to sleep. Sleep, he told himself. Maybe this time, he'd wake up in the right place, his own place, in his own bed.

Sammy was asleep when Kevin returned. Kevin's flashlight woke him. "Kevin?"

"Don't call me that." Kevin flashed the light in Sammy's eyes, then all around. "Don't call me that, never, ever." He lit a candle. "Call me that and I'll kill you."

"I'll never call you that," Sammy said.

"I hate the name Kevin."

"Me, too," Sammy said.

The wild kid untied him, then lay down on the mattress, hands hooked under his head. "Tell me that story again, how they put you out of the house."

"They pushed me out."

"Who's they?"

"My mom and Carl." Each time he said his mother's name he was glad. Kevin would know he wasn't alone. There were a whole lot of people waiting for him. His mother and his sister and Carl.

"Who's Carl?"

"My mother's friend." Sammy moved his hands up and down. He wanted words, more words. He wanted to keep talking, to say more things to Kevin, because it made Kevin not so scary.

"Carl's really my mom's boyfriend, but she says he's sort of like an uncle."

"Uncle!" Kevin snorted. "Is that what she said? What did they throw you out for? I bet you're a king-size, royal pain in the ass. You must have done something to get them going."

"I said a bad word."

"Bad word! How many bad words? Just one? What was it?"

When Kevin heard the word, he went, "Hoo-eee," and kicked his legs up in the air. He had an exploding, motor kind of laugh that never stopped. "Tell me more. This is really good. They kicked you out for that word? You want to hear some bad words?"

He said a bunch of bad words and threw himself around on the mattress, he was laughing so hard.

"You ever hear of K-Man?" he asked.

"Is that like Batman?"

"K-Man's like nobody but K-Man. He's here, he's there, he's invisible. He can turn himself into a tree or a rock, or disappear into the side of a building. K-Man will defend himself, no matter what. He'll fight a King Kong gorilla if he has to. K-Man never makes mistakes."

Suddenly he stopped, one hand raised. He gripped Sammy's arm. "Owww," Sammy said.

"Shut up! Don't move. Don't talk. Don't even breathe." He

blew out the candle, listened, then went out through the plastic curtain.

Sammy crept to the entrance on his hands and knees, and like a dog, he sniffed things, the trees and leaves and dirt on the ground. If he was a real dog, he could smell his way home.

"What are you doing?" The wild kid reappeared. "Did I tell you to stay inside or didn't I?" He slapped Sammy and pushed him back inside. "You gotta do what I tell you."

He flopped down on the mattress again. "Rats," he said. "That's all it was. They can sound like a whole army. What were we talking about?"

Sammy didn't say anything.

"They used to lock me up. In a closet, once, and another time they stuffed me in the trunk of a car. If they tried it now"—He sat up and slashed around like a karate fighter—"This is what I'm going to do, only they're never going to get me, because they're never going to find this place."

Sammy was silent.

"What's the matter with you?"

"I don't like being hit."

"Big deal." The wild kid swung at Sammy and stopped his fist an inch from Sammy's face. He hung over Sammy, his fist clenched, showing his broken teeth. "I could punch your face off. Nobody knows I'm here, nobody would guess in a million years. Nobody, till you came along with your dumb luck and fell right on top of me. Only a stupid kid would do that."

Sammy fell asleep sitting up while Kevin was talking, and when he woke, his head was sunk so deep on his chest, his neck felt broken.

Kevin was asleep. A square of gray light filled the window. Sammy crept carefully around Kevin, whose bare feet stuck out from under a blanket. Sammy got his head outside, and he was just putting one foot out when a hand grabbed his ankle.

10

All that long next day, everywhere that Kevin went, Sammy had to go, too. That, or be tied up. Any noise Kevin heard, he froze, and Sammy had to freeze, too. He couldn't talk. If he said a word, he was dead. Kevin didn't let Sammy out of his sight, even when Sammy had to go to the bathroom. "Over there, and cover it up. Go on! Kick some leaves over it."

Later, before Kevin went out, he tied Sammy up again. He didn't tell him where he was going or when he was coming back.

He didn't untie Sammy until the next morning. His wrists hurt all day. He was hungry and dirty. His shirt was torn, and his pants were filthy. His mouth felt funny. He asked Kevin for a toothbrush.

Kevin dragged him off to the little pool of water nearby and pushed his face in. "There's your toothbrush."

Sammy was crying. He tried not to cry, even when his hands and feet hurt from the ropes. "I'm not crying," he said.

That night, when Kevin went to tie him up, Sammy said, "Don't. I'll be good. I won't run away."

The wild kid hunkered in front of him, his hair tangled in his face. "Okay, what happens if I don't tie you up? And you go? The mosquitoes'll eat you up. Then you'll get lost. That'll be good. Solve all my problems. Get yourself lost out there, and when they find your skeleton, they can't blame it on me."

"I won't run away. I don't like the dark. I'll stay right here. I promise."

"Hmmmm. Hmmmm." The wild kid stared at him. Then he nodded. "Okay. We're going to give it a try." He threw a blanket at Sammy, then blew out the candle and left.

The moon shone through the window. Sammy went out to look. The moon was so bright, he could see the trees and the shape of rocks and bushes. He started walking home. It was wonderful to be free, to be moving. *You promised Kevin not to run away.*

He hesitated. A promise is a promise. What would his mother say? "Come home, Sammy." He took another step, and a mosquito found him. It bit him on the neck. Then a bunch of mosquitoes bit him all over his face. He ran back, slapping at his head and arms.

He dove into the cave and wrapped himself in the blanket. He pulled it over his head and stayed that way, afraid to open it even a crack.

11

Kevin was sitting on a rock, eating fries from a paper bag. They were the fat fries that Sammy loved. "Can I have some?" he asked. He was hungry all over. Even his legs felt hungry.

Kevin popped a fry in his mouth.

Sammy checked his watch. "It's time for me to eat lunch. It's twelve o'clock. Can I go home now?"

"Climb a tree," Kevin said. "I didn't invite you here. I don't have to feed you."

"I'm hungry. I'm very, very hungry."

"Go chase your tail."

The squirrels were busy in the trees. Nuts and leaves fell around Sammy. He picked up a nut and cracked it between his teeth, then tasted it. It was bitter. He took one step and then another. He made-believe this was the way home. He had to be careful not to get lost. Inside himself, there was a tight, scared feeling.

But he wanted to go home. He was going to eat and eat and eat. He was going to see his mother and his sister and be in his house, where he could open the door and go inside, and shut the door and lock it.

Ping! Something hit him on the cheek. *Ping!*

Kevin was above him, flipping pebbles at him. "You're going to leave without saying good-bye?"

"Can I go home now? I want to go home. Will you take me home now?"

"Shut up! You talk too loud." He pushed Sammy back into the cave.

Sammy sat down. "Can I talk now? First thing I want to say is, I'm hungry. The second thing is, I wish you had a TV." On weekends, when his mother slept late, he would watch TV until she woke up and made breakfast.

"Everything on TV is a lie," Kevin said. "It's all lies for boneheads like you."

"My mother says TV is good. She says you can learn from TV."

"It's a lie."

"My mother never lies."

"She lies. You're too stupid to know it. You lie, too."

"I don't, K-Man. I told you all the truth about me."

"Yeah? Tell me, are we friends?"

"I will be your friend," Sammy said. "Do you want to be my friend?"

"You're an idiot." Kevin bit into another fry.

"You sure eat a lot," Sammy said. "Can I have some now?"

"Do I look like a store?

"Can we go to the store?"

"Yeah, sure. You see a store around here? Where's your money?"

"You took my money."

"That was room rent." Kevin had the wild kid smile on his face, like he was waiting for Sammy to do something, and then he'd do something mean.

"You could give me some french fries, maybe five?" Sammy showed Kevin five fingers. "When I go home, my mother will pay you."

"Hey!" Kevin jumped up on his mattress. "Will she pay a reward for you? How much are you worth? What will she pay?"

"I don't know." Kevin was stupid sometimes. A person wasn't something you bought in a store.

Kevin brushed his hands off. "How much can I get from your mother? Are you rich? Are you somebody famous? Are you known?"

Sammy was confused. They weren't rich. It took a long time to get all the money for his bike. Remembering the bike made him feel really bad.

"How much money has your mother got?"

"I don't know. Fifty dollars." He wasn't good with numbers. "Is that a lot? Maybe not so much. She works hard." That's what his mother always said: "I work so hard."

"I'm going to sell you to the highest bidder."

"You can't sell me. You don't sell human beings."

"Who's going to stop me?" Kevin threw a fry at him.

Sammy caught it and ate it slowly. "Your mother would like that you're sharing," he said.

"My mother doesn't care if I'm alive or dead. Open your

mouth." He flipped another fry toward him.

He played that game for a while, until he got tired of it and tossed Sammy the rest of the bag.

All that day, Sammy waited for the wild kid to take him home. He couldn't imagine that he wouldn't take him home soon.

12

"Come on," Kevin said. It was late in the afternoon. He had his knapsack over one shoulder and a stick that he'd peeled and sharpened, like a fork with two sharp prongs. "My snake stick. I see a snake, I zap it to the ground."

"Are you going to take me home now?" Sammy asked. "I won't tell. It's a secret." He put a finger to his lips. "Sealed!"

"That, again? Don't you ever get tired of saying the same thing? Listen to me! Here's what your mother's going to say. 'Where were you, what'd you do, who were you with?' What're you going to say?"

Sammy pointed to his sealed lips.

"She's going to say, 'What's his name? The one who helped you?' What do you say then?"

"I'll tell her Kevin made me promise not to tell."

"Perfect," Kevin snorted. "Okay, let's go. Remember, I

don't leave trails. If you're going to leave a trail, leave an animal trail."

"A skinny trail." Sammy understood.

Kevin showed Sammy how to step over things, how to put one foot directly in front of the other. "Step and listen," he said. "And walk in my tracks."

He led the way up over the rocks. It was a hard climb. It was like climbing a mountain. The top was a wet, grassy place with a lot of dead trees. They were like tall people watching Sammy, the way his teacher watched him.

They went into the woods. "Don't take a step without looking back to see if you're leaving a trail," Kevin said.

"Step and look," Sammy said.

"Now you got it. I'm careful. If I sniff danger, I'm a tree. K-Man can do that. I go out when nobody's in the woods, in a storm, when the wind blows. I don't go out when there's snow. Then I stay put. I hibernate like a bear; I sleep a lot. Only when the snow melts do I venture out." Suddenly Kevin stabbed at the ground with his snake stick.

Sammy jumped. No snake, but after that, he couldn't step high enough.

They came to a cut in the woods with power lines running overhead. Power lines, Sammy thought, went to houses. Kevin must be taking him home! It was going to be a big surprise.

Kevin stopped near some bushes and pointed to a branch that was bent over and hooked to the ground. "Snare." He knelt down and adjusted a loop of twine.

"What's that for?"

"Catching rabbits."

"Rabbits? What for?"

Kevin looked into Sammy's face. "I eat them." He moved to another snare. He had a bunch of them.

"You eat bunny rabbits?" Sammy said.

"Yes, and you'll eat them, too."

Sammy knew he'd never eat rabbits. "Are you taking me home?"

Kevin wasn't listening. He was getting mad all over again. Every snare he'd set was empty.

13

There was no light, and Sammy didn't hear anything, not even Kevin breathing and muttering the way he usually did. "Kevin?" He pulled his blanket over his head. It smelled funny. Was he asleep or awake? Sometimes he was asleep and thought he was awake. Maybe Kevin was dead. Maybe there was no Kevin. Maybe an animal had chewed him up and would chew Sammy up next.

He made a big growly noise with his voice, then felt around and found a stick. Holding it made him feel braver. He sat with his knees up, and the stick ready. If a rat came out, he'd hit it on the head. He banged the stick down. It was good to have a plan. Plans made things better. That's what Mrs. Hoffman said. His plan was, sit up this way all night, and in the morning, if Kevin wasn't here, he'd find those power lines and go home. That was a good plan.

He was still sitting up, but asleep, when Kevin came back.

Kevin lit a candle, then dropped his knapsack on the floor. "Free food," he said. He pulled out a melon, some rolls, pieces of fried chicken, and other stuff. "Dig in," he said, taking a piece of pizza.

Sammy reached for the chicken. It looked like somebody had bitten into it, but it tasted good. He ate it all, then a slice of pizza, then he reached for the chicken again. He put a lot of food in his mouth, like Kevin. At home, he had to chew each mouthful with his mouth closed. And no grabbing. And you waited until you were served.

"This is good food," he said.

"It's garbage. Man, people throw away good food all the time."

"Garbage?"

"Yeah. You're eating garbage." Kevin wiped his hands on his pants. "Tastes pretty good, doesn't it?"

Sammy burped. "This is delicious garbage." He burped again. Then Kevin burped, a really loud one.

"I don't bring back everything. This is the best of it. Garbage can kill you, too. When I was a little kid, I'd put anything in my mouth. Once, I ate bad meat from the neighbor's garbage. I was four or five. I puked up all over myself, and the neighbor lady took me to the hospital. That was the time they took all us kids away."

"Where'd they take you?"

"Into foster care. I didn't even know what was good for me. I wanted to go back to my mother, I was that stupid." He put the remains of the food in the pizza box. "I think of her now, and depending how I feel, I'm sorry for her. Stupid cow. I don't know why I'm sorry. She never watched out for me, none of us. You heard of the old woman who lived in a shoe?"

"'There was an old woman who lived in a shoe,'" Sammy recited. "'She had so many children, she didn't know what to do.'"

"That's us. Except my mother wasn't so old. There was Karl, Kenny, Kelly, Kelsey, and me, Kevin. Kelsey came after me."

Sammy counted. "Five Ks," he said.

"That house was a wreck when we moved in, and we kids finished the job. There was this social worker who came to our house. She wouldn't sit down without looking behind her to see what someone had left on the seat. She told my mom if she didn't pull herself together, the kids were going to go in foster care again. So Mom cleaned up, sort of, and then my father came home, and we had a ball till all the money was gone. Then there was nothing to eat in the house but pretzels and Kool-Aid. I don't know why I'm telling you all this. Are you there?"

"I'm here," Sammy said. He was lying down and his eyes were closed, but he was listening. He thought about being taken away from his mother. No. His mother would never let him go. Besides, they always had food in their house, not just pretzels. He wished his mother was here right now. He wished it a lot. She would hug him, and then she would probably say something nice to Kevin. Then she'd say, "Time to clean up this dirty place, boys!"

14

Sammy decided it was Sunday. It was quiet like Sunday. No cars, no doors slamming. Quiet, except for the wind and insects and noisy birds. It seemed a long time ago that he'd lost his bike. A really long time. He could hardly think when that was.

Kevin was sitting against a tree with his face in the sun. His eyes were closed. Sammy practiced his steps. Step high. No stepping on sticks. No dragging toes. *Walk away now.* One step at a time. That was the way. One step, two steps . . . climb up rocks. Keep climbing. Climb till you come to the place with dead trees and snakes. But he'd better wait for Kevin.

He slapped at a mosquito. What if he stepped on a snake and got bitten and died? His mother would be sad. He pictured her in Bethan's room, standing by the window, where she could see the road and watch for him to come home.

He turned his face to where he thought their house was. It was where the sun came from in the morning. That was east. He learned that in school.

"I'm coming home, Mom. Pretty soon. As soon as I convince Kevin. Don't worry, Mom." If she saw him now, she'd be double worried. He'd lost his socks, his pants and shirt were torn, and he didn't have a toothbrush. And every minute he was missing school, falling behind. He'd never catch up unless he worked so hard, he would be tired all the time. He could do it. His teacher, Mrs. Hoffman, said he was a hard worker. She was wondering where he was, too. And the other kids in his class were saying, "Where's Sammy? When's he coming back? What a long vacation."

"Yeah, some vacation!" He slapped at another mosquito. Every day, mosquitoes! And every day, Kevin's food. He liked Kevin okay, although sometimes he didn't. Kevin said, "Sammy, you say one more word about going home and I'm going to pop you one."

How many days now? A lot. He started counting back. The day he lost his bike. That was one day. Then he slept in the woods, and then it was two days. And that was the day he fell on top of Kevin's house.

And then what? Oh, yes, he got it! All night, he was tied up. Kevin was mean then, but now sometimes he was nice, like showing him the snares and telling him about snakes. And then it was . . . three, four, five. He held up his hand, all five fingers. Five days. "Boy, oh boy," he said.

15

There was a rabbit caught in one of Kevin's snares. The first two were empty, but at the last one the grass was all flattened. The rabbit leaped into the air, but its hind leg was caught. Sammy felt sorry for it.

Each time Kevin reached for the rabbit, it sprang away.

Sammy hoped it would escape, but Kevin grabbed it. He pranced around, holding the rabbit by its ears. "What about that!"

"You're hurting it," Sammy said.

The rabbit cried when Kevin cut its throat. Sammy covered his eyes, but he looked. Blood bubbled up along the cut, like a black line drawn with a pencil. The rabbit's legs kicked and then they didn't.

Kevin hooked the rabbit to his belt by the hind legs, and they started back. Blood dripped on his pants. He stopped by a little stream. "Watch this," he said. "You're going to learn something." He gutted and skinned the rabbit. He threw the guts and the head away. It didn't look like a rabbit anymore.

When they got back, Kevin made a fire. Inside, he put a metal grate on some rocks. He bunched paper under it and lit it. The fire flared in the dimness. He sent Sammy out for sticks. "See if there's any smoke showing," he said.

"No smoke," Sammy reported, coming back.

"Never is." Kevin grilled the rabbit over the fire. "The way I did it, the smoke is sucked up through ten different holes in the rocks. Pretty smart, huh?"

When the meat was done, he tore it apart and told Sammy to dig in. "I don't eat rabbit," Sammy said.

"More for me." Kevin chewed on a leg.

Sammy didn't mean to eat it, but he was hungry, and it smelled so good. He tasted a little tiny piece. Then another piece, and then he couldn't stop. Nothing had ever tasted so good. When there was nothing left but the bones, he chewed them.

16

Sammy watched Kevin unwrap a candy bar with chocolate and nuts. He took a big bite and chewed. Sammy swallowed. He could almost taste the chocolate in his mouth. "Can I go home tomorrow?" he said. His mother would make him chocolate chip cookies.

"What for?" Kevin licked his lips. "They don't treat you so good."

"They do. They're nice to me," Sammy said.

"You call being kicked out of your house nice? What happens when you go back? Your mom's going to belt you. She's going to say, 'Why didn't you chain your bike?' That's right! And then Carl's going to kick your ass."

Sammy bit his fingers. Was Carl going to do that? He'd never hit him, but... Kevin was smart. He knew a lot of things.

"People aren't nice. They don't leave you alone. Somebody's always trying to make you do things you don't want to do, or they kick you or chase you. It's better here, in the woods."

"Trees watch you," Sammy said.

"Nobody squeals on you here. Nobody runs to the cops and says, 'There's this funny kid sleeping under the stairs.' I just went in this place to get warm by the radiator. And then this cop comes with the bracelets on his belt that he's going to snap around my wrists and drag me off someplace."

Sammy kept his eye on the chocolate bar. It was getting smaller and smaller.

"Then they want to know who I am and why and what I'm doing," Kevin went on. "Nobody's business but my own, but I don't say that. I jump out the window and run for it, then walk around the rest of the night till daylight comes and I can go in someplace and get something to eat."

Sammy listened. The candy bar had a silver paper lining.

"No, man. People are no good. They put you out of the house; you think that's nice? Your mother did that."

"Can I have a piece of that candy?" It wasn't polite to ask, but he couldn't help it.

Kevin broke the remainder of the bar in two and gave the smaller piece to Sammy. "Thanks!" Sammy shoved it in his mouth, then tried to make it last by sucking on it.

"Why don't you just stay here with me," Kevin said.

"Stay with you?"

"I don't care."

"Always, you mean?"

"Not the rest of your life, man. Just for now."

"Even in the wintertime?"

"It's not that bad. You go over to the mall and sit in the library."

"Is that far away?"

"What do you care? It's not that far. Nothing's that far away. Sometimes I help people with their packages and get some money. If it snows a lot, we stay here. Oh, man, I was warm, but once I couldn't get out for three days."

"Could I visit my sister and my mother?"

"What for?"

"I like my sister. I miss her."

"Look at me, Sammy. I don't have a sister. I don't have a mother, and I'm okay. You don't see me crying. I get along good."

Sammy thought about that. "So you would be like my brother, almost?"

Kevin shrugged. "Yeah, if you want me to."

"That would be good," Sammy said. "But I would still miss my mother and sister."

"What's so great about your sister, anyway? She's probably stuck-up."

Sammy swallowed the last bit of chocolate and ran his tongue over his teeth. "Bethan is not stuck-up. She's funny, and she helps me a lot. She teaches me things. She says if I keep practicing, I can learn anything."

"Yeah? How about those shoelaces? How come you can't tie your own shoelaces? Why didn't she teach you that?"

"It's too hard. My mother says—"

"See, that's what I mean. They're making a baby out of you. Here, give me that sneaker." He grabbed one of Sammy's sneakers and tied the lace. "Now, you do it."

Sammy tried, but it came out all wrong, as always, a big mess. "Boy, oh boy," he said. "I can't do that one."

Kevin studied him. "Are you trying, or are you just giving up? You want to know how to do it or don't you?"

"I do," Sammy said.

"Then pay attention. Are you watching?" Kevin knelt behind Sammy and guided his hands. He did it once, then he did it again, and again. "Now, you do it."

Sammy did it. "Is that right?" he said.

"Not perfect, but that's it. Try it again."

Sammy was surprised. After a few more times, he was doing it. He was tying his shoelaces. It wasn't any harder than swimming.

"Okay, buddy!" Kevin punched him in the arm. It hurt, but it was a good punch.

"Now let me punch you," Sammy said.

"Go," Kevin said, and Sammy punched him. "You call that a punch? Do it again."

Sammy did.

"Mosquito bite," Kevin said. "Baby touch. Come on, punch me hard. Draw your fist back. Turn sideways, and then let it go as hard as you can."

Sammy put everything into the punch. Whaam! Kevin fell down and lay still. "I'm sorry." Sammy leaned over him. "I'm sorry, Kevin!"

Kevin sat up and laughed. "You didn't do so bad for a beginner," he said.

17

"You're going to help me today," Kevin said. "You ready to work?"

"I'm a good worker," Sammy said. "What's the plan?"

"The plan is to make more room inside. We're going to knock down this wall." He touched the wall with the window in it. It was part of a big wooden packing case, disguised with branches on the outside. They pulled away the brush first, then slid the packing case out and propped it with rocks.

The inside was open now, on the side and on the top. Sammy looked up at the sky. "If it rains, we'll get wet." There were clouds in the sky. "Uh-oh, better not rain right now."

"Come on," Kevin said. "Stop talking."

Kevin cut down six skinny trees with a little saw, and they carried them back to the camp. One at a time, they set them between the packing case and the rocks. Kevin spread plastic over them and covered everything with a crisscross of branches, twigs, and leaves.

Sammy was getting tired and hungry, but Kevin wouldn't stop. He kept running from inside to out, looking at everything from different angles. "We have to camouflage it better," he said.

"I know what that means," Sammy said. "It's like army stuff. I have a camouflage suit."

"Cool," Kevin said.

Kevin moved rocks around to make the wall look more natural. When they got done piling brush against it, it looked like bushes growing next to rocks.

Inside, the room was big now. In back was the cave, and in front was a regular room. They arranged Kevin's mattress and Sammy's blanket next to each other. "Cool," Sammy said.

18

When the helicopter flew over, they were playing a game. Kevin had drawn a circle in the dirt. "You've got to aim," he said. "Hand-eye coordination. Watch me." He threw a small flat stone, and it fell perfectly into the circle. "That's ten points. If it lands on the line, it's five. Don't expect yours to be perfect. You've got to practice."

Sammy threw his stone. "Go in!" he ordered. It bounced outside the circle, then fell in. "Ten points," he yelled. "I got ten points. Yay for me!"

"That's a bouncer," Kevin said. "Bouncers get three." He threw again and missed completely. "Stop fidgeting!" he said to Sammy. "You threw me off."

When it was Sammy's turn, the stone landed just inside the circle. "Ten points! Ten points!" He was excited. "How many does that make, Kevin?"

"Count!"

Sammy counted under his breath. "Twenty!"

"You don't have twenty," Kevin said. "You've got thirteen."

Suddenly there was a clatter in the air, like someone banging on a giant tin can. A helicopter appeared just over the treetops. It had big white numbers on the side. Sammy started waving and shouting. "Here I am! Here I am!"

Kevin grabbed him and pushed him down to the ground.

"Let me go," Sammy said. "Let me go, Kevin. It's looking for me."

"Shut up!" Kevin punched him. He held him down till the sound of the helicopter disappeared. "You want to get me killed?" he said, releasing Sammy. "Blasting off that mouth of yours."

Sammy drew away from Kevin as far as he could and sat against the rock with his knees up.

"Okay, forget it," Kevin said. "You want to play?"

Sammy rubbed his arm.

"Come on, let's play. You're winning."

"No."

"What's the matter with you?"

"You don't hit your friends."

"Yeah, and a friend doesn't stab his friend in the back, either. Those guys come down here, you know what that means? That's me locked up again."

"You hit me," Sammy said.

"Oh, man, don't make a big thing of it. You know how many times I've been hit? Someone hits me, I laugh in their face. Everyone gets hit. That's life. Come on, forget it. Let's play."

Sammy wouldn't play, and he wouldn't talk. He was thirsty, but he wouldn't drink Kevin's water. Hungry, but he wouldn't eat Kevin's food. "I want to go home," he said.

19

"You talking to me yet?" Kevin said the next morning.

Sammy shrugged, the way Kevin shrugged. He could be tough, too.

"I got a surprise for you." Kevin had been going in and out all morning, looking through his boxes and pulling out clothes and putting them in his knapsack. "You want to know what it is?"

Sammy didn't reply.

Kevin put on the knapsack. "Come on."

"Where?"

"You'll see."

It was a hot day. They climbed the rock rubble above the shelter and Sammy was soon sweating. He was glad when they reached the dead trees and they were back in the woods again. He followed Kevin closely, swatting at the flies biting his neck. They crossed a trail and came out of the woods at the edge of a small pond.

"So what do you think?" Kevin said. "Is that a good surprise or not?"

"Good! This is good, Kevin." He loved water. He swam in the Special Olympics every year, and every year he came home with ribbons. He squatted down and put his hand in the water.

"Maybe we can catch some frogs," Kevin said. "You want to eat a froggie?"

Sammy shook his head. "No way, man!"

"You didn't want to eat rabbits, either. But you did, and it was good, huh?"

"No frogs," Sammy said. "Let's go swimming."

"You go," Kevin said, throwing the clothes he'd brought into the water.

Sammy shed his clothes and plunged in. The water grabbed him and soothed him. It made him happy all over.

As he swam across the pond, birds flew up out of the reeds. "Hello, birds. It's me, Sammy," he told them. "Don't be afraid."

He swam all around the pond, then back to Kevin. He was sitting on a rock with his clothes spread out to dry.

"Come on in," Sammy said. "Don't you want to swim?"

"No."

"Why not? Everyone likes to swim."

"Not me."

"It's not even cold anymore."

Kevin put a toe in the water. "Okay, I'm in. How's that?"

"All of you," Sammy said.

Kevin let himself into the water and dog-paddled around, staying close to the edge.

"You don't swim that good," Sammy said. "Put your face in the water. That's the dead man's float. Only you're not dead. And you kick your feet." He demonstrated, making a big splash.

Hanging on to a log, Kevin made a bigger splash.

"Want to swim to the other side with me?" Sammy said.

"Is it deep?"

Sammy let himself sink down. His toes touched mucky mud. He popped up. "Just a little deep."

"No, thanks, I'm staying right here. And if you get in trouble, I'm not going to save you."

Sammy swam around him. "Don't be afraid, Kevin."

"Hey, who's afraid?" Kevin let go of the log and took a couple of strokes.

"That's the way," Sammy said.

Then something happened. Kevin swallowed water and choked and started thrashing around. "I'm drowning!"

"Get on your back," Sammy said. "Turn over, Kevin! I'll help you." But when he got near, Kevin caught him and wouldn't let go, and they both went under.

Sammy kicked loose and popped up to the surface.

Kevin came up. He went down and he came up. His eyes looked crazy, and he went under again.

When he came up, Sammy was behind him. "Don't grab me," he shouted. He got hold of Kevin's hair. "Let me...don't grab." He pulled Kevin into shallow water.

Kevin staggered to the rock. He was coughing, spitting up water. He sat in the sun, shivering.

"I saved you," Sammy said.

Kevin pulled a towel around himself.

"You were learning to swim," Sammy said.

"Man, I was learning to drown." Afterward he sat on the rock, picking at scabs on his legs while Sammy swam back and forth across the pond.

20

"We're going on a special trip," Kevin said.

"Where? What is it? Tell me what it is, Kevin."

"You'll see. You'll like it."

"Because we're friends?" Sammy said.

"That's right."

Before they left, Kevin looked Sammy over and told him to wash his face. He gave Sammy one of his black T-shirts to wear under his jacket and watched while he tied his shoelaces. He wore a black T-shirt, too.

"Exactly two thirty-eight in the P.M.," Sammy said when they left.

"Perfect," Kevin said.

They went up over the rocks, but when they got to the dead trees, Kevin went a different way.

They came out of the woods in the back of a cemetery, where the grass mowers were kept. There was a garbage heap of clippings and discarded ribbons and empty flowerpots.

"If I say duck," Kevin said, "you duck. If I say run, you run. If I say don't breathe, you don't breathe."

Sammy practiced not breathing. He could hold his breath a long time.

They walked through the cemetery. A line of cars were parked along the curving road, and people were clumped together under a canopy. "Funeral," Kevin said. "That's good."

Were they going to a funeral? Was that the special thing Kevin had promised him? But, instead, they returned to the back of the cemetery.

"You wait here," Kevin said. "If anyone comes, just duck into the woods. Don't talk to anybody. Got that?"

Sammy nodded. "Got it."

"We're partners, right?" Kevin held out his hand, and Sammy slapped it. Kevin left his knapsack and jacket with Sammy and ran down the road toward the cars.

Sammy folded the jacket carefully on top of the knapsack, then sat down to wait for Kevin. The sun was shining, and the wind chased the leaves around in little circles.

Kevin appeared suddenly behind him. "Come on." He grabbed his jacket and knapsack, and they ran back into the woods. Kevin threw himself down on the ground and pulled a wallet from his pocket and another wallet from his other pocket. He took the money from them and buried both wallets under leaves. Then he led the way out of the woods.

Sammy followed. He was holding his breath, practicing swimming underwater. Or the dead man's float. Maybe somebody gave the wallets to Kevin. Some nice person who said, "Take the money and throw that dirty old wallet away."

They walked along the edge of the woods, past some big old buildings, then followed a long driveway to the main road. Kevin ran his fingers through his hair and tucked his shirt in. Sammy did the same. He looked at the pocket where Kevin had all the money. He knew nobody had given Kevin the money. Maybe Kevin was going to give it back someday. Or he would. He'd just go up to the person and say, "Sorry, my friend made a mistake."

There were six lanes of cars going in both directions. Sammy had forgotten there were so many cars in the world. He almost got dizzy. Cars, cars, cars. "Boy, oh boy," he said.

They went halfway across, then waited on the divider for a break in the traffic. On the other side, they ran across a half-empty parking lot to a huge mall. Buses were lined up in front of one of the entrances.

Sammy stopped to read the numbers. "One oh four. That's my bus," he said. "That one!"

Three boys sitting on a bench looked at him. "One oh four," one of them repeated. Sammy got a sick, scared feeling in his stomach. "Hey, baby!" they mocked. "Hey, one oh four. Here's your baby bottle."

"Hey!" Kevin glared at them. "Shut up!"

He made them stop. Sammy looked up at Kevin admiringly. "They were bad boys, weren't they, Kevin?"

"Jerks," Kevin said. He let Sammy hold his hand.

The inside of the mall was like a barrel of light and noise and big, echoey voices. Sammy hadn't been inside a real building in—how long was it? He started counting, then stopped to look and sniff. The smell of food made him dizzy.

In a bathroom they used the toilets and washed up. Sammy stood in the stall, flushing bits of toilet paper. A man was waiting to go in. "How about it, sonny?"

Sammy held the door open and smiled. "I'm done. Your turn." He washed his hands and face. He waved his hands under the faucets to make the water come.

"Okay," Kevin said. "Let's go. And keep that big voice down."

21

When they walked into the food court, Sammy wanted to start eating right away. Kevin bought egg rolls and fried rice from one counter, spaghetti and meatballs at another, and pizza and drinks.

Sammy kept sniffing the food. "Boy, oh boy, this looks good."

"Remember what I told you about your voice," Kevin said. He found a table in the middle of the room, and for a while, they just ate.

Sammy was too hungry to talk. He ate everything: spaghetti, meatballs, pizza slices, even Kevin's crusts.

Kevin leaned back in his chair. "What do you want next?"

"Pancakes and ice cream." Two women at a nearby table were throwing him smiles. He didn't think he knew them, but he smiled back. "I eat six pancakes every Sunday with maple syrup and butter. But this is the best meal I ever had in a long time."

"Hey, in your whole life, man!"

Sammy patted his belly. "Right, man!" He liked saying things the way Kevin did. It gave him the same good, full feeling that he had now in his belly from eating.

Kevin kicked his foot. "See that fat lady." He pointed to a woman at the bagel counter. "She could be my mother."

Sammy's head swiveled around. "Your mother?" What if his mother was here? One of the friendly ladies nearby looked sort of like his mother, except she had really short orangy hair. The other one had a big excited face. She was popping gum.

"What're you smiling at?" Kevin turned to look.

The two ladies were looking at them and whispering to each other.

"I think those ladies like me," Sammy said. His mother's friends always liked him.

"The whole world likes you." Kevin got to his feet. "Let's go, man." He took Sammy's arm and pulled him along.

"Where're we going now?" Sammy asked. He stopped at the ice-cream counter. "I think I want an ice-cream cone."

"Okay." Kevin glanced back. "But hurry it up."

Sammy ordered a cone with sprinkles. Just as the girl handed it to him, the woman with the orange hair tapped him on the shoulder. "Aren't you the boy whose picture I saw in the paper?"

Sammy smiled politely. Kevin was at the counter, paying. Sammy examined his cone for drips and licked them up.

"What's your name, honey?"

Before Sammy could answer, Kevin took his arm. "Let's go, Mike."

"Mike?" The orange-haired lady turned to the other woman. "Mike? Was that his name? I know I saw his picture. Let me get a look at you, honey. You look like that boy, the one who disappeared. Doesn't he, Connie?"

Kevin took the cone away from Sammy and tossed it away. "Move, Mike. Mom's waiting."

"Mike...Mike!" The orange-haired woman hurried after them. "Mike, is this your brother?"

Sammy nodded.

"It is?"

Sammy looked at Kevin and nodded again.

"Connie, see if there's a security man around." The woman held on to Sammy. "Is this boy your brother? Let me hear you say it."

"He just said it," Kevin said. "Let go of him." He pulled Sammy away. "Mom's waiting."

"Boys," the woman called. "Mike! Boys, just a minute, I'm not through talking to you—"

The boys went around a corner. "Run," Kevin ordered. They ran through the double doors and out into the parking lot.

22

It was dark in the woods, except for the circle of light made by Kevin's flashlight. Kevin was mumbling and talking to himself. "Stupid. Moron. Didn't you know what was going to happen? You didn't think. Stupid stupid stupid...."

"You're not stupid, Kevin." Sammy kept a hand on Kevin's shoulder. Every time Kevin said something, the flashlight went shooting all around, and Sammy couldn't see where his feet were supposed to go. "You're really smart, Kevin. You have a good brain."

"Did I have to go to the mall? Make the kid happy. Play the big shot. Couldn't I figure out his picture would be in the papers? How come I never thought of that? Dumb moron."

Sammy had never heard Kevin say so many bad things about himself. It happened when those ladies came. They kept saying, "Who are you? Who are you?" And Kevin said Sammy was his brother. Sammy didn't have a brother. He had two sisters, but if he had a brother, it would be Kevin. And his name wasn't Mike. That was funny. Would his mother be mad if she knew he said he was Kevin's brother Mike? He had to say it or Kevin would get in trouble.

If he saw those ladies again, he'd tell them Kevin wasn't really his brother. *I'm Sammy,* he'd say, and then the orange-haired lady would take him home. But where would Kevin go? They'd blame him because he didn't bring Sammy home, and they'd put Kevin in jail. And then Sammy would never see his friend again. So that was why he couldn't say his true name to those ladies.

He used to think only bad people lied. He used to think only bad people said bad words and stole things. He didn't want to think about it, but the thinking kept coming back. The same thing all the time. He didn't want to get Kevin in trouble, so he told a lie. It was bad to lie. He never lied. Only he did.

Then he had a new thought. If Kevin came home with him and lived in his house and slept in his room, and they ate together and went to school together—except, not to the same class—they would be really like brothers. Nobody would know they weren't, because if they lived together and did everything together, they were brothers, the way they were here, and then it wouldn't be a lie anymore.

23

"No," Kevin said. "It's a crazy idea."

Outside, it was raining. Inside, Sammy and Kevin were playing Go Fish, Sammy's favorite card game. It had been raining all day. Sammy kept thinking about being home. It was always dry in their house, even when it rained. But here, even when they were inside, it was sort of like being outside. The rain came in, not a lot, but sort of wet feeling.

Kevin had a can under a drip. Then another drip started. One drip went *ping! ping! ping!* and the other went *ping-pong! ping-pong!*

"Go Fish," Kevin said. "This is a stupid game."

"If you come home with me, Kevin, you can stay in my room," Sammy said again. "Friends are allowed to stay in my room."

Kevin got up and fixed the tarp. Then he went outside.

Sammy checked the fire. "Needs wood," he said, and went out for it.

When they came back in, Kevin flopped down on the mattress, and Sammy fed the fire. Then they continued playing. "If you come home with me, Kevin, we haven't got any leaks in our house, and we have a furnace. It's warm everyplace, except the garage. We can play in my room or the living room or the kitchen or anywhere, except the bathroom."

Kevin picked up a card. "That's beautiful."

Sammy had been thinking about his plan, but he hadn't said anything to Kevin until now. That was a mature thing to do. His mother would say so. *Think before you talk.* That was just what he had done. "My plan is this, Kevin—"

"Yeah, I heard your plan."

"This is my plan for you, Kevin. My plan is, we don't stay in the woods anymore. You come home with me. I'm home, and you're home."

"Go Fish," Kevin said. "I'm tired of this game." He got up and poked up the fire.

"Did you hear me, Kevin? You'll sleep in my room and everything. Did you hear my plan?"

"I heard it, Sammy, and it's not going to work."

"Kevin, it will. My plan is—"

"Sammy, listen to me." Kevin squatted next to Sammy so his nose was an inch from Sammy's nose. "One. Your mother would never let me live in her house. Two—"

"She will!"

"Two, three, and four and five, your mother will take one look at me and say, 'Out. I don't want you stinking up my house.'"

Sammy shook his head. His mother would never say stinking. She wasn't like that, anyway. When he'd found a sick kitty cat and brought it home, she fed it and took it to the veterinarian doctor. But it died, anyway.

He told Kevin this story, but Kevin got it all mixed up. "I'm not coming to your house to die," he said.

Sammy told him another story about the time his mother did something else good. She had a girl living with them who had no place to go. "She was alone, and her name was Irene, and she came from another country. See? My mother wants you to live with us."

Kevin emptied one of the cans outside. "Where do I sleep, in the cellar?"

"No, Kevin! In my room."

"How big is it?"

Sammy looked around. "Lots bigger than this. It has two windows. Two big windows and a bed and—"

"One bed? I'm not sleeping on the floor."

"You can sleep in my bed. I'll sleep on the floor."

"Your mother's going to love that. What's she going to say?"

"She's going to say, 'Sammy, you'll catch cold if you sleep on the floor.'"

"You've got it right. That's what I'm telling you. I can't go home with you."

"I'll bring in the pillows from the couch." His friend Billy Pryor had slept on the pillows one time when they had a sleep over and popcorn and a special video. "Do you like popcorn, Kevin? We can have popcorn every night."

"Is that what you eat in your house, popcorn?"

"No! Spaghetti and meatballs, and macaroni and cheese. And all the ice cream you want every night, after you eat all your vegetables. And pancakes on Sunday."

"I'll go for the pancakes. I don't want to eat with your sister, though, or that guy. What's his name? Carl."

"He doesn't eat with us, just sometimes."

"That's when I'm absent, man. I don't like old Carl. He's not going to like me, either. He sounds like a case. Anyway, who says I want to live in your house? Or anybody's house."

The more they talked, the better Sammy liked his plan. It was a good plan. Kevin was being very stubborn. He kept shaking his head and saying, "No way, man. I'm living the way I want to live. Nobody tells me what to do. Nobody gives me orders. Once you get out, you never want to go back in."

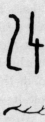

24

It was barely light when Sammy slipped out of the shelter. He carried his sneakers. He didn't want to wake Kevin and be called back. Outside, he put on the sneakers and a sweater Kevin had given him and tied his laces. He went up on the rocks, all the way up, zigzag, the way Kevin went. Without Kevin, the rocks were bigger and meaner, as if they wanted to stop Sammy. As if they were Kevin's rocks and not his.

He was sweating when he got to the top, but that was the end of Part One of his new plan. He wrapped the sweater around his waist. "Keep going, Sammy," he said. Part Two was find the power lines and follow them to a road. Maybe the road by the cemetery. Then he could go to the mall and get the number 104 bus. He would tell the driver that he lived on Pine Boulevard in Green Hills.

He could do things. Kevin said do it, and he did it. Kevin

let him use matches. He could make a fire and tie his shoes and wash his own clothes. And go home.

For a long time, it was trees and trees. Sometimes there were clear places, and he looked around hopefully for power lines. Mosquitoes attacked him, and he pulled his sweater over his head. It was hot like that, and he couldn't see so good. That was why he stumbled into a deep, sucky mud hole. It swallowed his sneaker and almost swallowed his foot.

"Wow! Boy, oh boy." He got his foot out okay, but he lost his sneaker and had to walk with one sneaker on and one bare foot. That was too hard, and he pulled the sneaker off and left it hanging on a branch. Barefoot was nice, especially stepping in all the wet, squishy places.

He kept looking ahead, expecting any moment to see the power lines. He ate some berries. His fingers turned purple. Every trail he came across looked like the right way, and then it didn't. "Not lost," he told himself.

A solitary tree stood like a giant among the other trees. It was like a crossing guard saying, "Sammy, come this way." He went to it, touched it. On the other side of the tree, he heard a humming like bees near their hives, or maybe ten million mosquitoes. He pulled the sweater over his head again and peered out through the holes. Ahead, the trees were thinner, and everything was brighter. He ran toward the light and came out of the woods.

In front of him, stretching as far as he could see, were rock cliffs. The humming was coming from the cliffs. It sounded like water, or a band playing one steady note, or . . . cars on a road. He looked up. He could almost see cars moving on top of the cliff.

He ran along the base of the cliffs, looking for a way up. In places, enormous sections of rock had broken loose and tumbled down. Sammy climbed to the top of one of these rockfalls, and then he couldn't go any higher. He sat down to think. The cliff went up and up, all the way to the top, where the road was. How was he going to get there? "You think hard, Sammy," he told himself. "Don't be a lazy mind."

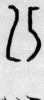

25

Sammy watched a line of ants move up the cliff, following a long, jagged crack. Black ants, like tiny bulldozers with pincers in front. His hand, wedged in the crack, was like a bridge for them. He blew the ants off, but they found their way back. Ants were smart. If he was an ant, he would climb straight up to the top of the cliff.

With his fingers and toes jammed into cracks, he inched his way along the cliff. His face, flat against the rock, felt like a pancake on a hot pan.

He kept moving sideways from one handhold to another. Here and there, trees grew straight out of the rocks, skinny but strong. They were good to grab on to.

From above a bird shrieked and dropped off a ledge, talons out, straight for him. Sammy ducked. Wings brushed by; he felt a rush of air. The bird flew out on rounded wings, shrieking again and again.

Sammy retreated, down and away from the ledge, then up another way. Stones and dirt spilled as he climbed higher on the cliff. Just above him, there was a little tree. When he reached it, he'd almost be on the top of the cliff. The tree had one branch that went straight out. He dug his bare toes into the cliff, stretched, and almost touched the branch. Reach a little higher. That was what Mrs. Hoffman had said. "Reach a little higher, children!"

Sammy took a breath and stretched as tall as he could, and caught the branch. It bent under his weight, and he hung there, feet bouncing against the cliff. He never looked down. Another breath. And he walked his feet up the rock, up and over the branch, and pulled himself into the skinny arms of the tree.

26

"Hello," Sammy called, and, "Hello" came back. "Hello, hello." And two hellos came back. The words in his mouth were like bubbles blowing out and coming back. Hello… hello…hello…hello…

"Help," he cried, and "Help" echoed back. His voice flew out and bounced off the cliff. *Help, help.* "Help, I'm stuck up here. Help me. Sammy's here." And the echo came back. *Here …here…here…* A lonely sound, which faded away to nothing. He felt more alone than ever. Nobody could hear his voice. Nobody would hear his voice.

He'd been in the tree for hours, the little tree with its one branch. He sat on Kevin's sweater, but his butt hurt, and his neck hurt from looking up, and his voice was sore from yelling so much. He checked his watch. It had been twelve thirty-four when he'd reached the tree. Now it was four-fourteen. Cars went by. Cars, cars, cars! Like a million bees saying the same thing.

"Somebody, look," he cried out. "Sammy's here! Somebody, come! Now!" He ordered the cars to stop. "Stop!" He put his hands out to block them, as if he could.

When he looked down, straight down past his bare feet, his belly shivered. Climbing, he'd been a little bit afraid of falling, but now he was a lot afraid. He looked down once. Then he didn't look down anymore.

He reviewed the plan. The plan was reassuring. The plan said, "keep going." The plan said, "Never give up, you can do it." It said, *"Keep going till you come to a road."* He had come to a road—almost. He just had to reach a little bit higher.

Again, for the ten millionth time, he stood carefully on the branch, balancing with both hands on the cliff, reaching for something to grab on to and pull himself higher. The cliff here was round and smooth and bulged out like a forehead, and there was nothing to grip. Nothing that would hold.

He stood as tall as he dared and called, "Hello, this is Sammy Ritchie talking. Hello. Help. This is Sammy. Help me."

Above him, cars swept by. He counted. He'd spent hours counting cars. He got to a hundred this time and stopped, then started again.

Only one car had to stop. Only one person had to look over the cliff. Only one person had to see him.

"Somebody, do you hear me? Somebody, stop this minute." He pointed his finger up. "Stop!" he commanded. Nobody stopped. Nobody looked over the edge. Nobody came.

He yelled and yelled until he couldn't yell anymore.

27

"Sammy..." The voice came from far away. "Sam...mee..."

He was sitting with his eyes closed, rocking in place and singsonging stories about his mother and Carl looking over the cliff and seeing him. "What are you doing there, Sammy?" They'd put down a ladder, and he'd climb to the top, and his mother would hug him and cry. Or maybe K-man would come leaping over the trees. Zooom! He'd land on the cliff, Sammy would climb on his back, and they'd zoom to the top and zoom to his house.

"Sam...meee..."

He came alert suddenly. He looked around and saw someone coming out of the woods. Kevin walked that way; so quick, you thought you saw him and then you didn't.

"Kevin..." his voice echoed. "Kevin, my friend!"

Kevin stood at the foot of the cliff, shielding his eyes.

"Look here where I am," Sammy yelled.

"What are you doing up there?" Kevin said. "I've been looking for you all day."

"I'm going home, Kevin." They yelled back and forth, and their voices echoed. Sammy pointed to the top of the cliff. "That way."

"I thought we were sticking together. I thought you were my buddy."

"I am, Kevin, but I have to go home first. I have to follow the plan. Kevin, I have a good plan. First, I go home. Then comes the best part, that's the secret part. First I go home, then—"

"Forget it," Kevin said. "You and your plans. I'm sick of hearing about it. Come on down now."

"I can't," Sammy said. "I can't come down."

"You got up there. You can come down."

"I'm afraid, Kevin. I'll fall. I'll break myself."

Below him, Kevin walked around and around. He stood under the cliff, then scrambled up the cliff.

"Come on, Kevin!" Sammy yelled.

Kevin didn't come fast. He came slower and slower, and he stopped a lot. Come on," Sammy urged. "You can help me get to the top."

Kevin stopped under him. He was pressed against the rock. His head was turned funny. "I can't come any higher," he said. He reached out a hand and so did Sammy, but they couldn't touch. "You have to come down, Sammy. Can you come down just a little?"

Sammy let himself down, with his arms hooked over the branch, till his feet touched nothing but air.

"Okay, get back up," Kevin said. "Go on! Be careful!"

He backed down the cliff, talking and talking. "Man, you did it this time! You're trouble, nothing but trouble. I spend all day looking for you. I find your sneakers up a tree and then I find you on the side of a cliff." He leaped down the last few feet. "You know what, Sammy, you're crazy! You're just a crazy kid!"

"I'm sorry, Kevin." Sammy sat very quietly. He made a sad I'm-sorry face.

Kevin kicked at a stone. "What do I care if you're sorry? Stupid, crazy kid! We had a good thing. You've ruined everything."

Sammy watched Kevin being mad. He went round and round in circles. He kicked and threw stones. "Kevin, are you mad at me?"

"No, I'm not mad at you."

"What are we going to do now, Kevin?"

"You're not going to do anything. You got something to tie yourself with? You got a belt?"

Sammy shook his head. "Just your sweater that you gave me."

"Okay, put the sweater around yourself and tie the sleeves around the tree. Do it now."

Sammy did it. "Are you going away?" he asked. Kevin was walking toward the trees. "Kevin! Where are you going?"

"You just stay there and don't move," Kevin shouted. "Don't try anything."

"K-Man, are you coming back?"

Kevin kept going, disappearing into the trees.

Sammy was alone. He was all alone. He pressed against the tree. All his life, people had helped him. He was Sammy

E. Ritchie, a special person. But now, no matter how loud he yelled, even if he yelled the loudest he'd yelled in his whole life, it wouldn't matter. It was all up to Kevin. Maybe he would come back, and maybe he wouldn't.

28

Sammy watched the night creep across the face of the cliff. It was like a big dark hand coming closer and closer. The cars sounded closer, too, louder and faster.

The sun went away, and the air got cold. He'd tied himself to the tree with Kevin's sweater. Above him, car lights splashed against the dark sky.

When he was little, Sammy had said the sun belonged to him. It rose for him, it was his sun, and when it set he wanted to know where it had gone. But in school, Mrs. Hoffman had taught them how the earth went around the sun, and how sometimes it faced the sun and sometimes it turned its back to the sun. He learned it, but in his heart, he still felt the sun was his. Now, it had left him. It was lost in the dark, the way he was lost, afraid the way he was afraid.

* * *

He dreamed they were all in the kitchen now. Mom and Bethan and maybe Carl. He put himself in the picture, next to Bethan. Kevin, too. But they only had four chairs. They'd have to get one more from Bethan's room. Carl and Mom would sit on one side, and Kevin would sit next to Sammy. They'd all hold hands and say grace before they ate. Then Kevin would tell them about the adventures of K-man and Sammy, and make everyone laugh.

A light woke Sammy. It was shining down from above, swinging back and forth along the cliff. "Sammy?" Kevin's voice was close. "Sammy, are you there?" The light went this way and that.

Sammy couldn't see Kevin, only the circle of light, but that was Kevin behind it. He had come back. His friend Kevin had come back.

"Sammy, somebody's coming, you just hang on. I've got to go now."

"Don't go away, Kevin. You're going to live in my house."

"You take care, buddy." The light went off.

"Kevin? Shine the light, Kevin." Sammy kept staring at the spot where Kevin had been, waiting for the light to shine again.

When the light came, it exploded across the whole cliff. And then a strange voice said, "Sammy, this is Officer Rosenberg. Sammy, can you hear me? Say hello, and I'll tell your mother you're okay. I've got her on the phone. Say hello, Sammy."

"Hello," Sammy said.

29

People in yellow helmets were lined up along the top of the cliff. A crane appeared, popping out suddenly like a long-necked bird, and then a bucket descended slowly toward Sammy. He waved, and two men in yellow helmets in the bucket waved back. "I'm Richard," the one holding a walkie-talkie said.

"I'm Chris," the other one said. "Sammy, just relax, we're going to get you out of there. You sit still and let us do everything. Okay, Sammy?"

Richard spoke over the walkie-talkie. A second line came down with straps attached to the end. Richard caught it and swung it over toward Sammy. "Catch it, Sammy, but don't reach."

Sammy nodded. He was so tired.

He missed the line the first time, and Richard swung it toward him again, and he caught it. Richard told him how to put on the harness and where to snap it across his chest.

Sammy was lifted free and swung out from the cliff. There was nothing under him, nothing to hold on to but the rope. He flew up over the cliff, over a clump of cars and people.

Then he was down, and hands reached out and held him. A policewoman hugged him, and he hugged back. "How are you feeling, Sammy? I'm Officer Rosenberg. Do you hurt anywhere?"

"I feel hungry."

"Anybody have something for the kid to eat? Crackers? Candy bar?"

Lights were flashing, and cars were backed up along the highway. Two men and a woman appeared with a stretcher. "No food till he's checked," one of the medics said.

They put Sammy on the stretcher, blanket over him, and loaded him into the ambulance. The policewoman and one of the medics got in back with him. "Where's Kevin?" Sammy asked.

"Who's Kevin?" the medic asked.

"He must mean the kid who called us," Officer Rosenberg said. "He's around someplace."

Sammy tried to sit up. "Where're we going? I have to wait for Kevin."

Special to the Post-Standard:
SAMMY COMES HOME!

Twelve-year-old Sammy Ritchie was back in his own bed last night, after being lost for thirteen days. Friends and neighbors were jubilant, and an impromptu party was held on Pine Boulevard in the Green Hills section of the city. The smile on Sammy's face never faltered. "Am I glad to be home?" the boy who characterizes himself as "a special person," said. "Boy, oh boy, I am glad."

His mother and his two sisters, Bethan, a fifth grader at Green Hills Elementary School, and Emily, a student at the University of Vermont, never left his side. "I never, ever gave up hope," Mrs. Ritchie said. "I knew I'd get my boy back."

Sammy was rescued from the side of a cliff at the edge of Middleburg State Forest Preserve at six-thirty A.M. after an anonymous caller reported seeing him there. Sammy was barefoot and hungry, and when asked how he'd gotten as high as he had on the challenging cliffs below Highway 104, he said, "I climbed and climbed. I climbed really good."

Pete Nelligan, the Preserve Manager, was doubtful. "Nobody but an experienced rock climber could get that high on the sheer rock face," he said. He speculated that the boy may have stumbled over the cliff in the dark and miraculously grabbed on to a tree and saved himself. For hours, cars passed above him, unaware that a child was trapped there.

When asked how long he was on the side of the cliff, Sammy consulted his wristwatch. "A long time," he said. "My butt was sore, and I was real hungry."

The boy was taken first to Chase Memorial Hospital, where he was checked by doctors and declared to be fit, although he'd lost some weight, according to his mother, who was with him when he was released.

Sammy, who has Down's syndrome, disappeared without a trace two weeks ago on a rainy Sunday afternoon. He went out to play and rode away on his bike. When he didn't return home by supper time, his mother called the police, and a search ensued, which quickly became statewide. Four days ago, the governor himself participated in the search. "I have a boy, too," he said.

Sammy's bike was found three days after his disappearance. Jim Terrance, who lives on Ten Mile Road, was found riding it. He says he found it in a ditch. Sammy says he left the bike, unlocked, in front of Marsden's Market on South Bay Road when he went in to buy a candy bar. "Stupid me. I forgot to use my special chain that Carl got me."

He says he chased after the thief and, in a series of escalating incidents, ended up lost in the forest preserve. That area of Middleburg State Forest Preserve is characterized by deep gorges and rocky cliffs and is of great interest to geologists and local rock-climbing enthusiasts.

Sammy says he found another boy in the forest, a boy living wild, who took care of him. According to Sammy, they lived in a cave and survived on rabbits and berries. When asked who the boy was, he refused to give his name, but rescuers state that he repeatedly asked for "Kevin." Despite an extensive search by the authorities, no trace of a "wild boy" was found. Dr. Ruth Hurt, a psychologist, explained that children of Sammy's mental abilities often fantasize and create a safe "world" of the imagination for themselves when they are in difficult situations. "It's a terrific survival mechanism," she said.

Carl Torres, a friend of the family who participated in the search for Sammy for each of the thirteen days, said, "I don't know about this fantasy stuff, but this is one heck of a brave kid. He went through an ordeal and, look at him, he's got more heart than ten people."

But questions persist. How could a child with no wilderness skills and who has Down's syndrome have been able to survive two weeks of exposure? Although he lost some weight, the doctors pronounced him fit. Perhaps Sammy's mother, who knows him better than anyone else, was correct when she said about her son, "He's more resourceful and smarter than people think."

Sammy agreed. "I can do things," he said.

30

"What I can't forgive him for is not letting you go that first day," Sammy's mother said. They were all sitting around the table, his mom and Carl and Bethan, just the way Sammy had imagined, but no Kevin. He kept looking out, thinking maybe Kevin would be coming.

"They were thirteen totally horrible days." His mom's eyes got all teary. "I thought I'd lost you. Do you remember that I hit you?

"Mom, you don't have to talk about that," Bethan said.

"Yes, I do. I'm so sorry. Do you still feel bad, honey?"

He shook his head.

"I don't know what I would have done if you hadn't come back."

"I'm back." Sammy went to his mother and hugged her. He wanted to tell her not to cry. He wanted to say it was not so bad, not all the time. Scary things happened, but mostly it was just things happening to him that had never happened before. "We killed a rabbit," he said.

"Did you really eat it?" Bethan wrinkled her nose. "How can you eat a bunny rabbit?"

"You can, if you're hungry enough."

Carl was nodding his head. "That's right. You get hungry enough...."

"He should have brought you right home," Sammy's mom said.

"A friend would have done that," Carl agreed.

"He took care of me," Sammy said. He didn't like it when his family criticized Kevin. "Kevin is my friend."

"It was good that he took care of you," Carl said. "I'll give him credit for that. And he went for help. That was a big thing. A little late on the uptake, but..."

"A *little* late!" his mother said.

When Kevin came, Sammy thought, his mother would find out how good he was. He was only bad sometimes. Not all the time. Sometimes bad, sometimes good. Mostly good. Like Sammy, he was two ways, too. Everybody was two ways. Carl wasn't just one way. Even his mom wasn't always good.

"Just because you're not always good doesn't make you bad," he said.

Carl and his mom looked at each other. "The kid's got a point," Carl said. "I couldn't have said it better myself."

When Sammy brought the folding cot from the garage into his room, his mother helped him move it in. "Your room is too small for another bed," she said, but the cot remained because Sammy wanted it there. When he woke in the morning, the first thing he did was look over to see if Kevin had come yet.

He had put a string of Christmas lights in his window so Kevin would know which room was his. And he kept the window ajar at night so if he was sleeping when Kevin came, he could climb right in. He knew Kevin would come at night. He didn't like going out during the day.

"All you talk about is Kevin," Bethan said. "Is he a real person?" She sat down on the cot. "You can tell me."

"He's real, Bethan. Kevin is my best friend. He's going to live with us in our family."

"Some of my friends say you made him up. The wild kid! They say it was something you saw on TV."

Sammy gave a big laugh like Kevin, like K-Man. He made his hands into fists. "Ha-ha-ha!" He pointed to his shoes, the laces tied. "He taught me that. He taught me, Bethan. He held my hands and did it with me a million times. He said, 'They baby you!' He said, 'You can do this, Sammy!' And I did it, and—"

Bethan made the time-out signal in front of his mouth. "Okay, okay, I believe you."

"Wait till Kevin comes. You'll see. He'll tell you himself."

"Does he know where you live?"

Sammy hadn't considered that. It worried him till he thought of the telephone book with their name in it. "Kevin will call me up," he shouted at Bethan.

She put her fingers in her ears. "I hear you, Sammy. Does he have a telephone?"

Sammy thought that was very funny. "No! No telephone. No toilet. No TV." He looked around his room. "No lights. No beds. No bureau. No desk. No chair. No toothbrush. No...no—"

"Time-out," Bethan yelled. "Okay, he'll call you from a pay phone. What will he say?"

"He'll say, 'Hello! Can I talk to my friend, Sammy?' He'll say, 'I'm coming to visit you.' No, not *visit*. Live! He's coming to live in our house, in my room."

"But you said he lives in the woods."

"He does, but it's a secret place."

"Is he there now?"

"I don't know," Sammy admitted. It was one of his worries. Where was Kevin now? Why didn't he come? What was taking him so long?

31

Sammy wrote Kevin a letter.

Dear Kevin,
I want you to come. I fixed the room.
You have a bed and I have a bed. No
sleeping on the floor. I have everything
ready. Come soon. Thank you.
Love, Sammy

His mother saw him writing. She looked over his shoulder. Sammy covered the paper with his hands.

Since he'd come home, his mother wanted to know where he was and what he was doing every second. She watched him from the window. But, why? He wasn't going to get lost again. He wasn't going to leave his bike without his special chain. He wasn't a baby anymore. He did things. He didn't have to be watched every minute and be asked about everything.

"Who are you writing to?" his mother asked.

"Private."

"Private?" She laughed. "I didn't know we had private secrets. Can I see?"

"No."

She looked at him. "You've changed. You've become very stubborn."

"I am a stubborn person," he agreed. He remembered himself on the cliff. The way he'd gotten up there, and the way he'd stayed there and waited. He hadn't cried once. "Don't baby me anymore," he told his mother.

"But you are my baby. My special baby."

"I'm almost thirteen years old. I do things. I can make a fire. I can walk in the woods. I'm a great swimmer. I can do things, Mom. I saved Kevin from drowning."

"I know you can do things," she said. "I know you can, and I'm proud of you. I'm so glad to have you back." She hugged him, a big one, and he hugged her back.

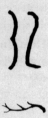

32

Sammy wished he had a picture of Kevin to show his mother and his friends in school. The kids in his class kept saying, "Where's Kevin? Where's the wild kid? We want to see him."

"When's he coming?" Lauri Bower asked. She was his new girlfriend.

"I don't know, but I hope he comes soon," Sammy said.

"Are you going to bring him to class?"

"You bet. Boy, oh boy, I sure will."

"Will there be a party?" Lauri asked. She was pretty. She'd just had her thirteenth birthday party, with thirteen candles, plus one for good luck.

"For sure!" Sammy said. "A party for Kevin." Kevin had never had a party. "This will be his first party ever," he said.

"Then he can only have one candle," Lauri said. And everyone laughed at the thought of a wild kid with only one candle.

Sammy wanted to tell Kevin the joke. He kept saying it to himself so he wouldn't forget. There were a lot of things to tell Kevin when he came, more than he could hold in his head.

So he wrote Kevin another letter. He didn't know where to send this letter, either. The mailman didn't deliver letters to trees in the woods. That was another joke to tell Kevin. He kept the letters in his desk. It made him feel good to write them. It was almost like talking to Kevin.

At night, Sammy would often stand by his window, looking for Kevin, looking to see if he was out there somewhere in the dark. He had the cot ready for Kevin and a pair of big pajamas folded up under the pillow.

Sometimes he talked to himself, the way Kevin would talk. "Trouble, trouble. That guy is nothing but trouble. I'm waiting for him. And where is he?" And he'd shrug, the way Kevin shrugged.

He remembered things they did together and how he saved Kevin from drowning. Kevin was scared, but Sammy said, "Don't be afraid, I'll save you." And he did. And then he remembered how Kevin saved him, how he came to the cliff and said, "See you soon, buddy. Take care."

"See you soon, buddy," Sammy said to the night. "Take care."